The Berenstain Bears
NO GIRLS ALLOWED

Is it so important that
He and she-bears aren't the same
When what really matters is
How we play the game?

A FIRST TIME BOOK®

Bears
ALLOWED

Random House 🏠 New York

Copyright © 1986 by Berenstains, Inc. All rights reserved under International and
Pan-American Copyright Conventions. Published in the United States by Random
House, Inc., New York, and simultaneously in Canada by Random House of Canada
Limited, Toronto.

Library of Congress Cataloging-in-Publication Data: Berenstain, Stan. The Berenstain
bears : no girls allowed. SUMMARY: Annoyed that Sister Bear always beats them at
baseball and other "boy" type activities, her brother and the other male cubs try to
exclude her from their new club. [1. Sex role—Fiction. 2. Brothers and sisters—Fiction.
3. Clubs—Fiction. 4. Bears—Fiction] I. Berenstain, Jan. II. Title.
PZ7.B4483Bfe   1986   [E]   85-18246   ISBN: 0-394-87331-9 (trade);
0-394-97331-3 (lib. bdg.)

Manufactured in the United States of America   7 8 9 0
                                                     C D E F

Ever since Sister Bear had been a tiny cub, she liked to tag along and play with Brother Bear and his friends. It was a bit of a nuisance because she slowed down their running . . .

"Wait for me!"

interfered with their climbing . . .

"Not so high!"

and messed up their marble games.

"Oh! That slipped!"

But as she grew older, things changed. She still liked to tag along with her older brother and his friends and it was no longer a *bit* of a nuisance: it was a BIG nuisance. She got to be a fast runner and outran Brother and his friends.

"Look at her go!" said Papa.

She got to be a good climber and outclimbed them.

"Oh, dear," said Mama. "I do wish she'd be more careful."

And she won all their marbles.

"Goodness! I hope they're not playing for keeps!" said Mama.

"It certainly is good to see Sister and Brother and their friends playing so nicely together," said Papa. "Look, they're organizing a baseball game."

"Yes," said Mama. "But it does worry me just a little that Sister is the only girl in the group."

"Now, Mama," said Papa. "It's not whether you're a he or a she that counts, it's how you play the game—look, she just hit a home run!"

"I agree," said Mama. "But think back—how would you have liked it when you were a cub if some little girl could outrun, outclimb, and outhit you?"

Papa thought for a moment.

"I wouldn't have liked it," he said.

Brother and his friends didn't like losing either. And what made it worse was the way Sister celebrated every time she won.

Her victory dance and cartwheels were annoying, but it was the war whoops that really got on everybody's nerves.

Then one day, when Sister was planning to tag along as usual, her playmates were nowhere to be seen.

No matter, she thought, and went about her business. She picked wild flowers for Mama and jumped rope with some butterflies.

When there were no
cubs around the next
day, she was puzzled.

But there was plenty
to do—she had a tea
party for her dolls and
read some books.

But on the *third* day she began
to wonder what was going on.
"Where *are* those cubs?"
she said aloud.

They weren't in the
old climbing tree.
They weren't
playing marbles.

And they certainly weren't
on the baseball field.

As she stood on the deserted field
wondering where everybody was, she heard
voices. They sounded like cubs' voices,
and they were coming
from the thicket.

She followed the sound into
the thicket. What *were* those cubs
up to? When she reached the edge
of Frog Pond she found out!

What they were up to was building a
secret clubhouse on Berrybush Island
in the middle of Frog Pond! It had
peepholes, watchtowers, and a little
bridge—it was almost like a castle.
What a wonderful surprise!

"Hi, gang!" she shouted.

She was so excited that she did her celebration dance, complete with cartwheels and war whoops! But Brother and the other boys didn't answer Sister's happy cry. Instead they ducked inside, then reached out and put the finishing touch on their new clubhouse: a sign that said "Bear Country Boys Club—NO GIRLS ALLOWED"!

As Sister stood there trying to think what to do next, there was a creaking sound. The bridge was a *drawbridge* and they were cranking it up! She was heartbroken.

"It isn't fair!" she wailed as she ran home from the thicket.

Bear Country Boys
NO GIRLS
ALLOWED

"You're absolutely right!" roared Papa.
"It *isn't* fair! Come, we're going back
there and *make* them take you into their
silly club—and if they don't, I'm going
to tear that clubhouse limb from limb!"

But Mama stopped them. "I don't think that's the answer," she said. "Those boys *are* being very unfair. Sometimes boys act that way— so do girls—but whoever does it is wrong. The important thing is not whether you are a boy or a girl, but the sort of person you are...

"And, be that as it may, you can't *make* cubs want to play with you."
"No," said Sister, "but you can
tear them
limb from limb!
Come on, Papa!"

"Wouldn't it be a better idea," suggested Mama, "for you to form your own club and build a secret clubhouse of your own?"

"Could I?" said Sister.

"This old climbing tree might be a good spot for it," said Papa. "And I'll help!"

"Terrific!" said Sister. "The first thing we'll need is a big sign that says 'NO BOYS ALLOWED'!"

"No," said Mama. "The first thing you need for a club is members."

That part turned out to be easy.
News of the No Girls Allowed club
traveled fast, and there were quite
a few other sisters who didn't like the
idea of being left out. They had a lot of
good ideas. Lizzie made a rope ladder that
they could wind up when they didn't want
visitors. Ellen brought a spyglass
for keeping watch. And Marsha had
the best idea of all—a tin-can
phone system.

With Papa Bear's help they built a very fine clubhouse high up in the old climbing tree.

"Now for that sign!" said Sister. "Those boys were just being mean because I outhit them and won all their marbles! They're bad losers!"

"I suppose that's true," agreed Mama. "But you know, there's such a thing as a bad winner, too—someone who makes a big braggy show every time she wins." Sister Bear knew exactly who Mama was talking about.

"But it still isn't fair," Sister said.

"Well," said Mama, "I think we can work things out. But first we have to celebrate the opening of this very special clubhouse with some very special refreshments: barbecued honeycomb and salmon!"

Now, if there's anything cubs are crazy about, it's barbecued honeycomb and salmon—girl cubs... *and boy cubs*. So Papa loaded up the barbecue.

The yummy smells reached
into the thicket and floated
right under the noses of
the members of the Bear
Country Boys Club...

. . . who followed their noses back to where the members of the Bear Country Girls Club were just pulling up their rope ladder.

"Something sure smells good," said Brother, speaking into the phone. The girls took a vote and decided to invite the boys up for honeycomb and salmon.

"How would you like to come back to our place for dessert?" said Brother. "Our berry crop is ripe for picking."

"Love to!" said Sister, and while
the whole gang headed for Frog Pond,
Brother ran ahead and quickly
changed the clubhouse sign to say
"Bear Country Boys Club—GIRLS WELCOME"!
The berries were delicious.